The Tannery

Sherrie Hewson

PAN BOOKS

First published in paperback 2009 by Pan Books
an imprint of Pan Macmillan Ltd
Pan Macmillan, 20 New Wharf Road, London N1 9RR
Basingstoke and Oxford
Associated companies throughout the world
www.panmacmillan.com

ISBN 978-0-330-46434-5

3 5 7 9 8 6 4 2

A CIP catalogue record for this book is available
from the British Library.

Printed and bound in the UK by
CPI Mackays, Chatham ME5 8TD

**To my daughter Keeley and grandson Oliver,
and to my brother Brett and my mum Joy**

The Tannery

Sherrie Hewson has been an entertainer since she was four years old. She went to the acting school RADA at 18 and has appeared in films, TV, theatre and on radio. She is perhaps best known for her roles in *Coronation Street* and *Emmerdale*. Sherrie has been a presenter on ITV's *Loose Women* for the last seven years.

Sherrie was the winner of the TV series *Murder Most Famous*, hosted by famous crime writer, Minette Walters. In the show, celebrities competed to be chosen to write a Quick Reads novel and this book is the result.

The Tannery is Sherrie Hewson's first book.

The Tannery

Chapter One

I was brought up in a small village in the north of England. Our street was long and narrow and the houses were joined together in a terrace. Each house had two stone steps up to the front door. Everyone kept the steps clean and white by polishing them with a donkey stone made from sand and cement. We would take old pots and clothes out to the rag-and-bone man with potato peelings for his horse. He gave us donkey stones in exchange.

Everyone took such pride in the appearance of the outside of their houses. Woe betide anyone who didn't keep their bit of pavement swept, and let the street down. Door knockers and letter boxes were polished to a high shine. The windows were washed with hot water and vinegar and dried with brown paper. Net curtains hung at all the windows and were kept beautifully white. They were useful to hide behind when the tally man came to collect money due, and to twitch when spying on the neighbours.

When I was small the doctor's man would come every Friday to collect his payment. There was no NHS in those days, so you had to give money each week as a kind of insurance to pay the doctor in case you got ill. Most families couldn't afford to do this, so instead the women used all sorts of home-made remedies. Camphorated oil was popular and used all year round. If you had a cold one of your dad's socks would be soaked in the oil. Then the sock was tied round your neck and fastened with a pin. Your vest would also be soaked in the oil, and then you'd be sent off to bed. Cod liver oil was used as a prevention and a cure for almost every ailment. At school we'd be made to line up, and one by one we'd be given a deadly spoonful. If you were sick, you were given another dose straight away. Diphtheria, polio and TB were the killers in those days just before the Second World War. Child mortality was very high.

Winters were cold; summers were stinking hot. The houses had no insulation to keep them warm in winter and they were never cool in summer. We used to leave the front and back doors open for the breeze to blast through. We had a cold tap and a water barrel to catch the rain in the back yard. The water would freeze in the winter months and become stagnant in the dry hot weather.

We never had much money but it didn't seem to matter. All the kids loved the long summer days. We girls tucked our dresses in our knickers so we could move more freely. The boys wore short trousers, had scabby knees and always had snotty noses. Their mums spat in their handkerchiefs and used them to clean the boys' dirty faces.

The boys played marbles. I loved marbles – they were so pretty – but I had nothing to swap for them, like football cards or conkers. My favourite game was hopscotch. You drew a grid on the pavement with chalk and numbered the squares. Then you threw a stone into the grid and hopped on one leg to get to the square so you could pick the stone up. If you stepped on a line you were out. I was never quite sure what I was doing, but the older girls used to let me join in.

There was also skipping, but this scared me.

Two people turned the rope and you needed courage to jump into the middle. They'd sing as they turned:

'The big ship sails on the ally–ally-oh,
The ally-ally-oh, the ally-ally-oh.
The big ship sails on the ally-ally-oh,
On the last day of September.'

I'd rock backwards and forwards in time with the rope, but I was too afraid to run and jump in. Instead, I'd watch the other girls. One, two, one, two. As the rope went up they'd run out again to shouts of glee. Not me.

When dusk started to fall, the lights came on in the houses, casting shadows on the cobbles, giving them faces. In winter the chimneys smoked, warm coal fires beckoned and the smell of cooking wafted over us. Our tummies rumbled and the chill evening air nipped at our faces, and we'd drift off into our own homes. There was always a bit of shoving and pushing and kicking from the boys. I'd stand on our doorstep till the last kid had gone in waving at no one and singing softly, 'The big ship sails on the ally-ally-oh, the ally-ally-oh . . .'

*

We lived at number 26 Pevril Street. I loved the name Pevril, because it sounded like Bovril, my favourite drink. I had it at bedtime instead of Ovaltine. Had I known it was made from cows, I'd have been sick. There was a tannery just up the hill from where we lived. This is where they cured cow hides, scraping meat and fat from the animal skins – 'chucking-up time' we kids called it, because it stank. My dad worked there, but he would never talk about it. 'It comes out as leather' is all he would say. We were none the wiser.

Two of the older boys on the street, Billy Taylor and his brother Terry, from two doors up, told us stories about the tannery. They said the cows were skinned alive.

'If you listen carefully,' they said, 'you can hear them screaming.' Later I realized these were just horror tales made up to scare us, but I believed them at the time. I had nightmares where cows' faces stared at me, pleading to be saved. I cried and cried for those forgotten trapped creatures, little knowing that the future held the same horrors for me.

Chapter Two

Mum and Dad were my whole life. My mum was a real live wire, as Dad would say, full of life and laughter. She was a pretty woman with lots of red curly hair piled up on her head. And she had ringlets which would fall, one by one, down the back of her neck and over her forehead. I loved her hair and wished that mine was the same colour.

I had pale blue eyes like my dad, but my mum had large dark green eyes, a sweet nose and full lips. Dad called her buxom. He said she was a fine figure of a woman which meant she got a lot of attention from men and loved it.

They went out to the Royal British Legion every Friday night.

I'd sit on a stool in her bedroom and watch her get ready. She was so beautiful. She started with her foundation garment – a tight corset 'to hold it all in'. She couldn't afford stockings, so she stained her legs with tea. Then I'd draw lines up the backs of her legs with her eyebrow pencil. I became quite good at it. They looked like the real thing.

She talked all the time. Told me stories about how she wasn't really going to the Legion. Instead, she was being whisked off to a port and would be boarding a liner and sailing to America. She laughed and said not to worry because she'd come back for me. Then we would both sail away on the boat and dine with the rich people. She promised to buy me a yellow silk dress and yellow satin shoes.

In my mind, I've sailed on that boat so many times.

Mum and I had a nice relationship. Not close and cuddly, but I liked her and I wanted her to like me.

The last part of the ritual came just after she'd done her hair. I'd be in bed, waiting, with my hands over my eyes. She'd knock on my door and say, 'I'll be leaving now.' As she walked in I'd lower my hands and look at her, all dressed up to the nines. She always wore a red dress which swished round her calves as she flounced up and down my room. She had little black gloves and a long black coat with a fur collar.

But what I loved most of all was her hair. It would be swept up on the right side with a comb. All the curls tumbled down the left side. Even though there was only one ear showing, she still wore two fake-diamond earrings.

These were my happiest moments. She'd walk to the door in her brown suede court shoes, turn and blow me a kiss. 'Catch it, Doll,' she'd say, laughing. 'Watch the bed bugs don't bite.' And then she'd be gone. I'd lie back and dream of us on that great big liner sailing away to America.

My dad was a mild-mannered soul, quite tall and thin with a black moustache. I hated the moustache because it tickled. To me he was the handsomest man alive. He had pale skin which tanned very easily in the sun. He always smelt clean, like carbolic soap. But his hands were stained by the red dye they used at the tannery. It looked like dried blood. He had hard calluses on his palms which made his hands rough to touch.

When they went out Mum was always

nagging him. 'Put your hands in your pockets, Wilf. I don't want people knowing you work up at that tannery. You always stink of dead cows. At least make the effort to look like you're somebody, for God's sake. Not some cheapjack common manual worker.' I hated her doing that.

Dad never answered back. He'd smile at me, lighting a Woodbine. 'You see, princess? Can't do right for doin' wrong.'

When I look back, I wish I'd been older and could have stood up for him – then maybe things wouldn't have ended as they did.

My favourite times with my dad were in the evenings. We had a wireless and it was a special treat for me to be able to listen to it. I'd sit on his knee enveloped by his safe arms. The fire would be warm and the shows were funny. We'd laugh and laugh. Mum used to say we were crazy. Eventually I would fall asleep and he'd carry me to bed.

That's a memory I try to hold on to, though it slips further away as the years pass. They say we look back at our past through rose-tinted glasses. That's possibly true, but when your world turns upside down and the harsh reality of life hits you, then those glasses aren't much use.

Chapter Three

My world started to change when the war came in 1939. I remember grown-ups becoming very serious. Many of them spoke about 'the Germans'. The boys told us girls that 'the Germans' were the 'enemy'. So we all had to be prepared, because they would try to invade England and they were very bad and very ugly. There were cartoons of them everywhere. Funny-looking soldiers with scared faces and tin hats being chased by our brave British soldiers. They looked pretty frightened to me.

At first it was an exciting time for us kids. The adults were all busy and we had free rein to run riot. We sang 'Run, rabbit, run, rabbit, run, run, run' as loudly as we could while the boys marched up and down the street pretending their mums' yard brushes were rifles. The boys played soldiers all the time: Billy, Terry, Arthur and a thin lad called Stanley. Everyone used to push Stanley around because his dad was the undertaker and they thought it was funny. I always felt sorry for him, but I was too shy to say anything. We girls were busy with our dolls and pretend shopping and making pretend tea.

I never thought it was fair that in the boys' games the Germans always died. I thought they should take it in turns. I expressed this opinion to all and sundry, which often resulted in a clip round the ear. But I didn't know any better. We never had anything explained to us.

'Children should be seen and not heard.'

'Don't speak until you're spoken to.'

'You're just a squirt. What do you know?'

This was the reaction to a 'cheeky kid with too much front'. Then you got a clout.

In 1940 the Blitz began and bombs started falling on London. I sat with Mum and Dad, in silence, as we listened to reports on the wireless about what was happening. What was it like for the kids who had bombs landing in their streets? Then it was our turn and we found out. Luckily, we weren't bombed too badly. The school was hit, but most of the kids were thrilled about that.

*

My father left for the war in August 1941 when I was nine. He said he was going away to 'teach the Germans a lesson' and to tell them never to come near England. 'Over my dead body,' he told me proudly. He said they were evil and Mr Hitler would murder us all in our beds. I assumed that was why Mum and I stayed under the stairs when the air-raid sirens sounded, so Mr Hitler wouldn't find us.

Nearly all the men in our street went off to the war except for daft Raymond's dad, who had one leg shorter than the other. Once the men had gone, life changed for all of us who were left behind. I never forgave my dad for leaving me.

Although Mum had complained about it, my dad's tannery job had paid very well. 'Because no other bugger would do it,' my mum said bitterly.

To help subsidize our rations she took in washing and did the odd cleaning job on Mount Street. That was where all the nobs lived. I would sometimes go with her, just to see the inside of those big houses. I wanted to look in every room and feel the beautiful clothes. I particularly hoped to see the bathrooms. Mum had told me that they didn't have tin baths like ours. She said their baths were made of porcelain and were clean, white and bolted to the floor so no one could move them. She also said the bathrooms contained toilets that had a chain you pulled and everything disappeared.

I knew she must be fibbing, so I wanted to see for myself. But despite my best efforts, every time I got to one of the houses I was kept out of the way. I used to have to go and sit in the servants' quarters till Mum had finished work. The very last time I went with her, I was feeling really ill: I had a bad tummy and a hot head. As I sat on a chair in the kitchen I felt freezing cold. Jane, the scullery maid, brought me a cup of hot tea. Normally I loved this. I could pretend, with my proper cup and saucer, that I lived in the house. Or imagine that I was at a posh hotel having high tea. Fish and chips on plates, not wrapped in newspaper.

But when she handed me the tea, I threw up all over her. What was worse, I dropped my lovely teacup and saucer and the cup broke. Jane screamed and the rest of the staff peered through the door.

The cook, Mrs Skittles, hurried in. Horrified, she shoved me out of the back door into the frigid air.

'You're a bad lot! Take that nasty bug home. Comin' here infectin' my Jane, you dirty little toe rag.' Muttering on, she slammed the door in my face and then bolted it.

I walked up the back stairs to the street and waited for my mum. I was scared that I'd be in trouble.

She came out about ten minutes later with a look as black as coal. Not a word was spoken between us, and she walked home with such determination and not a glance in my direction. My wanting to be sick and feeling so hot was overtaken by fear.

When we got home we went into the kitchen and, as I was taking my coat off, she started shouting at me. I could see her shaking with anger. She said I was stupid. If only she hadn't taken me with her. Mrs Skittles had told her she had to pay for the broken cup out of her wages and to get her snotty sick kid away from the house. But the worst thing was that she was never to come back, there were no jobs for the likes of her. Suddenly, she lashed out at me, slapping me across the face. It really shook me. We both stopped dead. She stared at me, her eyes cold yet shocked.

Tears came to my eyes, but they only made her more angry. 'Don't start that. Do you think I wanted to be lumbered with a kid? Your dad wanted children, but I never did. I never wanted any of this. It's all because of you I ended up marrying your good-for-nothing father. Now look at me! Get out of my sight,' she screamed. 'Get out!'

I ran out of the kitchen. As I started up the stairs to my room I could hear her sobbing. It was such a lonely sound I wanted to go back, but I felt afraid. Sometimes now, I wish I had.

I prayed and prayed for my dad to come home. I thought he'd make it all better. I also prayed to God to punish those people in the big houses. He must have heard me because Mount Street was stripped of all its fancy iron railings and big black gates. They were taken away for the war effort, and it didn't look quite so pretty and posh then.

Chapter Four

By 1943 lack of money had become an ever-increasing problem. There was little food and no new clothes. We could barely afford the rent. When I turned twelve my mum took me out of school to help her. Most kids left school about that age anyway. 'What's the point of staying on?' Mum said. 'You've got all the learning you need; it's money we want now, not bleedin' books.'

These hard times had changed my mum. I so wanted to see the happy, laughing, stylish woman who used to throw me a kiss and say, 'Catch it, Doll.' On the odd occasion I'd hear her singing quietly in her room. Once, when I was about to go downstairs, I heard her muffled voice and I peeked through her slightly open bedroom door. She was standing with her nightie on and a grubby old fur wrap of her mother's that she'd had for years. In one hand she was holding a small battered suitcase, and in the other she had a large drink. She was looking in the mirror, as if she was imagining herself going on holidays, maybe on a big liner. I wish I had realized earlier how much alcohol was part of her life. I could have helped.

Without Dad's pay packet we just about managed to get by. Although Mum had lost her cleaning job, she still had the washing and ironing she took in. I collected bundles of dirty clothes from all over our neighbourhood.

Two sisters, Phyllis and Polly Birtles, lived in the end terrace and Mother said I must get them to give us their washing. 'They've got a bob or two. You can tell by their shoes,' she said.

So one day I knocked on their door. It opened slowly, and out of the house came the smell of baking.

'Yes?' It was Polly, I knew, because everyone said, 'Polly is puny and Phyllis is fat.' Not fair, I know, but that's how people distinguished them.

'Do you have any washing please, Miss Polly?'

The little white-haired lady stared at me. She had on a pretty full-length flowered dress and was wearing brown brogues on her feet. She was so tiny I was looking down at the top of her head.

'Come in, come in.' She pulled me into the kitchen, calling, 'Phyllis, come and see our visitor. She wants to wash her hands. She's lovely, Phyllis.'

A tall, much larger lady came into the room from the yard, also dressed in long old-fashioned clothes.

'Stop, Polly. Sit down.' She sat her in a large comfy armchair. The room was warm and clean and on the kitchen table was a golden-brown pie.

'Sorry,' I said, 'I don't want to wash my hands. I wondered if you wanted any washing done.'

'My sister's shop was bombed and it has left her totally deaf, among other problems,' Phyllis boomed. 'We had a lady who did our washing, but she doesn't come any more, so that would be very helpful, thank you.' With that she handed me what looked like clean tablecloths and towels.

As I was leaving Phyllis took my hand.

'The war has affected all our lives in different ways,' she said, 'but we mustn't judge people. We must always be there for them when they need it.' I couldn't imagine what she meant, but she seemed very kind, so I just smiled at her. As she turned to go back inside, I saw Polly hanging on to her skirt like a very small child.

Mr Cricket lived opposite Phyllis and Polly. He always sat outside his house on a stool with his pipe and Blackie his Labrador. I never spoke to him because his face was really crumpled, so he looked very angry all the time. But now I plucked up my courage.

'Mr Cricket, me and my mother are taking in washing. Do you need any doing?' As I got nearer to him I could smell something very bad. 'Mr Cricket?' I said again.

'I 'eard you. Do I look like I need any washing doin'?'

I didn't know if that was a question or not. 'Well, yes, you do,' I said.

He laughed so hard that he almost fell off his stool and Blackie wouldn't stop barking.

'Fer your bloody cheek you can 'ave it.' He chortled. 'Follow me.'

When we got inside the house the smell was worse. I noticed dirty clothes all over the floor. He bent down and began to pick them up one by one, shoving them into my arms. Each time he bent over he broke wind and I realized that was the smell! Mr Cricket turned out to be a good customer, despite the stench, so I went back to him every week.

Often when I got home, our neighbours were outside their front doors, fags in hand. Joan lived on one side of us, Mary on the other. They would watch me carrying the heavy bundles of laundry up the road to the house, but never attempted to help. 'Where's your mother? In bed as usual?' Joan sneered at me one hot morning, and they both collapsed into laughter. I didn't understand them, but I knew they weren't being nice.

Each week I'd spend hours boiling water on the range and pouring it into a large washtub. Then I'd pound the clothes until they were clean. The sheets were fed through the mangle over and over again, squeezing every last drop of water out. It made my arms and back ache and often I caught my fingers in the press.

Some of our neighbours tried to help when they could. Mr and Mrs Beadles owned the greengrocer's. Mrs Beadles was a decent woman. I loved to walk by her shop. Although there was a war on and food was in short supply, the display outside was always colourful. There were lots of sweet red and green apples, big knobbly potatoes, dark green cabbages and rhubarb which was a lovely fading pink. There were carrots as big and orange as you liked. And there were beans and peas in their pods. They were such a joy to pop and eat raw.

'What have we here?' Mrs Beadles would say. 'A bag full of goodies going to waste.' Then she'd hand me an assortment of vegetables that would make a soup for the rest of the week.

There were about ten families I collected laundry from. One family, Armitage the Funeral Directors, was in Century Road. Mum had told me to try them because they had money. 'With all them dead bodies,' she said, 'they're bound to want some washing doing.'

Their son Stanley was the boy I used to feel sorry for when I was at school. He was still at school and still teased badly. They said he was puny and thin because his father made him sleep in a coffin. He was lonely and sometimes I noticed bruises on his arms. Once when I was passing their yard to go to Mrs Beadles', I saw his dad swipe him across his head but I never told a soul.

We hadn't heard how Dad was. We didn't get letters or money posted back to us like the other families. I wondered if this was because my dad couldn't write.

Mum never mentioned him. I had tried to talk about him once. I started to tell her that I missed him, but that I was proud too. I knew he was fighting for all of us. But she was having none of it.

'Don't you know what's happening?' she said. 'He's left us to manage on our own. He could be sending us money, but where is it? What do you think? That he's saving up a big fortune and will come back to spend it all on us? You need to wake up, girl. It's you and me now. We're on our own.'

I couldn't bear the thought of my father never coming home. 'You're wrong,' I said, 'don't ever say that. I couldn't stand it without my dad.' Then, realizing what I'd said, I went towards her. She shoved me away and I tripped and fell backwards, banging my head on the range. As I started to cry she said, 'Where's your daddy now? Not much comfort, is he?'

As time went on, she seemed to be drinking more and more every day. She spent less and less time at home. Most of her time was spent at the pub. The house was a mess and sometimes when I came home there was a nasty, stale smell. I grew to hate that smell. I'd walk through the door and start to wipe and clean before I'd even taken off my coat. The washing and ironing started to pile up and I'd try to do as much as I could before I got too tired.

She would stumble in from the pub and get angry to see me working. I couldn't understand it. Each time, somehow, I thought she'd be pleased and each time she was cross. 'You think you're so good, don't you?' she'd start. 'Look at you, Miss Bloody Goody Two Shoes.' Once she picked up the ironed laundry and started to throw it round the kitchen. I watched her undo all my hard work and tried my best not to cry.

And so we went on. Me trying hard to keep things clean, she getting more and more angry the more I tried. Sometimes I got a backhander for my trouble. If I had bruises I would stay indoors, or Joan and Mary would have had another good laugh at my expense. But I hated having to hide inside. I felt trapped. And the funny thing was, I couldn't feel angry with her. I knew she felt trapped too.

Her only escape was the booze. I tried to hide some of our money from her. Otherwise she drank it and we had nothing to eat for days. If she caught me, she belted me for being a thief. I became quite good at lying.

There were sometimes good days. Then I'd see something of the mum I had known before the war. She would be in her room humming to herself. One particular day she called to me. As I walked in, for just a second, I saw her as she used to be. She was spinning round in her slip, and she had stockings on and a pair of old but nice shoes. She was holding her hair up and it was flying everywhere.

'Come here, Doll.' She grabbed me and we

both spun round and round. As we span, we began to laugh, our laughter getting stronger the faster we twirled. She slowed down as she started to cough. Stumbling towards the bed she reached out to steady herself.

'Get my dress, Doll.'

It was an old print one she'd had for years. I helped her on with it. As she was bending down I noticed her hair was going grey at the top. The dark red was beginning to fade. She moved over to look in the mirror. Her face was bloated, her cheeks were brightly flushed and her eyes were dull.

'Go and wait for me downstairs,' she said, suddenly sharp. I looked at her. 'I've got business to do and you're coming with me.'

We went out together across the recreation ground. As we paused at the top of our street my mum looked up towards the tannery and its plume of dark smoke.

'The wind's in the wrong direction,' she said sadly, as we got a blast of curing cow hide from the tannery. 'It smells of death.'

Chapter Five

When we went to town with our ration books, Mum flirted brazenly with all the male shopkeepers. Especially with the butcher, Mr Doby.

I thought him an ugly man. He was round and short, always dressed in white with a long blood-stained apron. He was red and sweaty and reminded me of the pigs that were hung up in the back of his shop.

When we walked into his shop one day, he dashed out from behind the counter, kicking up clouds of sawdust off the wooden floor. He whispered in Mum's ear and she laughed. We waited until Mr Doby had served all the other customers and we were left alone with him. He wrapped up a piece of meat and put it on the counter. Then he put his arm round Mum's waist. He glanced at me, but she laughed again. Suddenly, he grabbed her and pushed his body against hers. She pulled back, as if teasing him.

'You come round later,' she said, picking up the meat from the counter. 'I'll pay you then.' She placed her finger to his wet and greedy mouth.

He leered at her. 'You certainly will.'

She pushed me out of the shop and slammed the door behind her. There was a dark look on her face and I knew not to speak.

Mr Doby did come round for payment, as did many other men. My mother referred to them as my uncles. It meant we ate and paid the rent. Mother looked older every day and the light in her eyes went out.

Things were never the same. I cooked, cleaned and did the washing. I ran the house and kept out of her way. The only task I really hated was clearing up in her room. I did it every morning, being careful and quiet so as not to wake her. I always hoped that whoever had been with her that night would have gone by the time I went in.

There would be empty bottles lying about

and cigarettes stubbed out on the floor. The smell was terrible: sweat, beer and men's stale breath. Sometimes Mum would be lying naked across the bed like a dead cow waiting to be taken away. At other times she would be curled up under her blankets like a baby. I'd clean her up, wrap her in her dressing gown and sit on the bed stroking her hair as she clung to me.

'Let's leave here, Doll,' she'd often whisper. 'Let's go somewhere pretty, start again? You, me and Dad.' Half asleep she'd start to cry. 'You're my life, Doll, you're the only one who loves me.' Then she'd fall asleep.

That was how our days passed.

On the nights when she didn't go out drinking, she'd sit in her chair by the range and stare into space. I wanted to hug her and tell her it was all right, that we would get through. One day we would go away on that big liner and dance and sing, and she would be beautiful again. But I knew, really, that it was too late.

Chapter Six

In 1945 the war finally ended. There was such joy on people's faces and hugging and kissing every time you went out into the street. Even though most of our neighbours hated my mum because they all knew what she had become, and hated me for being her daughter, they still grabbed us. 'It's over,' the women cried. 'They are all coming home.'

My mum just stared at people. I knew instantly what she was thinking. She was wondering what had happened to my dad – was he coming home? I was excited and nervous at the same time. We hadn't heard anything about him since he'd gone. Was he even still alive?

Everyone else was joyous and celebrating. Over the next few weeks we all waited hopefully for our loved ones to come home.

Some families still got the dreaded telegram saying 'Killed in Action' or 'Missing, Presumed Dead' as the events of the war caught up with the people at home.

I used to watch my mum sitting by the fire rocking backwards and forwards. Sometimes she would be silent. At others she would make a slight humming noise to the tune of 'The Big Ship Sails'. Was she dreading Dad coming home or was she terrified he would be dead and then all we would have was this, she and I, this life?

Then the truth of the situation hit me. How terrible for him to come back and find out about the life she had led. But would he find out? The neighbours would be sure to tell him. Joan and Mary would relish it. I watched her and felt sick. She couldn't live with herself whatever happened. I knew she was praying for the telegram saying killed in action.

Nine months after VE day and we'd given up hope that he'd return. I really believed my dad was never coming back.

One evening we were sitting by the fire, listening to the radio. There was a loud knock on the front door, which startled us. The front door was never used. When anyone did come round they would come to the back door and walk straight in.

'You go,' Mum said, and I knew why. I sometimes had to handle an angry wife or a man who wouldn't take no for an answer. It always scared me.

Once Mr Jackson the pub landlord had come round. It was after closing time. He hammered on the front door, having found the back door locked. The neighbours were leaning out of their bedroom windows swearing at him. He was getting angrier and angrier. Mum sent me to pacify him. He was a tall, heavy-set man with a large belly bursting through his shirt.

I opened the door and he pushed past me, stinking of smoke and beer. 'She isn't here,' I told him. He pushed me out of the way. 'You're a liar, girl,' he shouted. 'Your whore of a mother owes me! She's not paid her dues for weeks.'

'She's away, at her sister's,' I lied. 'I'll bring the money round in the morning.' He made a grab for me, but I ducked under his arm. As I started for the stairs, he grabbed my sleeve and dragged me towards him. I bit him, hard.

'You little bitch!' He pulled back from me. 'Tell your mother I'll be back tomorrow.'

With that he was gone. I lay on the floor, sickened, wondering what might have happened to me.

I opened the door a crack and, in the half light, saw the silhouette of a tall, frail-looking, khaki-clad individual hovering outside. What should I do? I shut the door. There was another knock.

'Who is it?' Mum barked. She was not in a mood to be messed with.

'Just going,' I called back to her.

I turned the handle and pulled the door open.

A soldier stood there, his head bowed.

He lifted his head and an old man stared at me. The face was familiar. I peered at him.

As my dad wept on our doorstep, my heart felt it would burst.

Chapter Seven

I ushered my father in and took his coat and kit, dumping them on the floor, then led him into the kitchen. He had finally come home and I never wanted to lose him again.

Mum didn't look up. She was in her normal place slumped by the range. I realized what a mess she was. I wished I'd known my dad was coming home. I'd have cleaned her up and made her pretty, like she used to be.

'Mum, look who's here.'

There was a flicker of her eye.

'Make some tea then,' she said gruffly. I could see she was shaking.

Dad sat at the table as I busied myself. He was silent. He looked like he couldn't believe he was in his own home.

We had tea together – as a family. We barely spoke. That night, as I collected a blanket and a pillow from my room to make up a bed for Dad in the front parlour, I heard my mum sobbing in her bedroom.

From that moment on, I tried even harder to create a happy family home, just as it had been before the war. I made sure the house was scrubbed and that there was food on the table. I tried to bring us all back together.

My dad would wander from room to room in a sort of daze and my mum kept out of his way.

After a time they began to talk to each other. They both stayed at home. And I began to notice a change in Mum. She did her hair, was always clean and tidy and smelt good. I carried on taking in washing, but I knew that wouldn't keep us in food much longer. The money wouldn't be enough for the three of us. I held my breath, hoping this was a new beginning and everything else would be forgotten.

Then one day I was out collecting washing from Mrs Dainty. She was anything but dainty at four feet ten and about as wide. She had wispy red hair fading to white with bald patches. She had no eyebrows so, instead, she'd pencilled them in, in dark brown. Her bosoms seemed to hang to her waist and she smelt of wee. We had just come out of her front door and she was bundling more washing on top of the already enormous pile. It was full of her six kids' dirty underwear. She only had them washed once every four weeks.

'Your dad's not looking good,' she said with a sly smirk.

I turned to get away, but she held on to my arm. I caught a whiff of her eggy breath.

'Let's hope no one talks about you know what,' she whispered with a snigger. 'Now that'd kill him, never mind the war.'

I watched her go back inside, my heart sinking. My worst fears had been voiced by that fat old bag. Someone, sometime soon, was going to tell my dad what my mum had been doing while he was away.

Mum never ventured out at all now. Dad had started to go for walks and go to the pub occasionally. I dreaded him coming back, having been told about what had been going on. But, for some reason, nobody said anything to him.

Maybe everyone thought we'd been through enough. Fat chance.

One afternoon, Dad came home in a jolly mood. 'I've got my job back,' he announced proudly.

I was out in the yard and Mum was upstairs lying down. I poked my head round the door. 'What did you say, Dad?'

He swung round. 'I've got my job back at the tannery. It's not the same money, but it's a job.'

I could understand his pride. Work was hard to come by.

'I thought you never wanted to go back there,' I said cautiously. 'You said you couldn't work with the smell of dead animals, and you know Mum hates that place. Dad, why don't we go away from here, start again somewhere new?'

'Hey, what's this? Move? Start somewhere new? We can't do that. There's no money, princess.'

He hadn't called me princess since his return; I felt my heart swell. But I was also worried. Mum really hated the tannery. I knew she wouldn't think Dad's job was good news.

As if summoned by my thoughts, she suddenly came into the room.

I drew in a breath. There, in front of me, was a different woman. Her hair was washed and swept up, just as she used to do it. Her face was clear, with a little lipstick and a tiny hint of rouge. She wore a pale blue dress with primroses round the collar and a pair of pretty white shoes.

It was an old outfit and a bit worn, but it didn't matter. She'd tried.

Dad turned to her. 'You look a picture, lass.'

He was smiling from ear to ear. He moved towards her and for a moment I thought my mum blushed. It made me want to cry; to forgive and forget everything that had happened between us.

Dad reached down to her and, as time seemed to stand still, he gently kissed her.

That image of the two of them standing in the doorway will be imprinted on my mind for ever. It was the only time I really saw what could have been.

Dad looked lovingly at Mum. With obvious pride, he said, 'I've got a job.'

My heart sank.

'A job?' Mum asked.

'Now, I know you won't want me to do this, but it's all there is at the moment. Times are hard. Maybe later something else will come along.'

She shook her head. 'No, no, no. Surely you're not going back to that dreadful tannery.' She turned to me with pleading eyes. 'Dolly, tell him. He can't go back there. We've got to leave here. Make a fresh start.'

I didn't know what to say to her. Dad sat her down on the chair by the range. He stroked her hair, tried to calm her.

'I know that times must have been hard. There was me in a prison camp. Couldn't send any letters or any money. But you managed. You both did well. We can't just walk away from here. We haven't got anywhere to go to. Besides, this is our home. You have all your friends round you.'

He stood up and kissed the top of her head. 'Now, let that be the end of it. I'd like some peace too.'

As he turned to go, she looked up at him with hate-filled eyes.

'Friends round me?' She stood and walked towards him. 'You really think I'm going to stay in this stinking hole any longer? While you were off trying to be a hero, we nearly starved! Do you actually think we managed on taking in other people's filthy washing?' She got angrier and started jabbing him in the chest. 'You think you can just walk back in here and behave like the bleedin' master of the house? Well, let me tell you how we really survived.'

I grabbed my dad, who was standing in stunned silence, turned him round and pulled him out of the kitchen.

'Go, Dad! Go for a walk. She needs to calm down. You don't know this side of her. She doesn't know what she's saying. Please, leave her to me.'

He looked at me with such sad eyes and walked out of the house like an old man.

I went back to the kitchen to find her standing staring out of the window. She was talking to herself so quietly, I could only just hear her.

'If he thinks I'm staying here, after all this, with these people round here,' her voice started to rise, 'he knows nothing, Doll, does he? "Times have been hard." He'd know that, would he, the stupid bugger. He's no different than before. The war hasn't made him into a man at all. He's still a wimp. A job at the tannery? He'll fit right in. He's just like one of those poor dead cows. That's about all he's good for. Scraping the flesh off dead animal skin. Does he really think I'd sleep in the same bed as him smelling of death?'

I put my hand on her arm, trying to calm her, but she spun round, full of rage.

'You, you did nothing, you just stood there! You always were a daddy's girl. You never liked me, did you, Doll? Were you going to tell him about your naughty mum?' She grabbed my chin. 'Well, were you?'

'No, of course not.'

'You can if you like. Tell him about the men in my bed. I need a *man*, a man, like Dan Jackson. At least I got a few drinks out of him.'

I didn't know what to say. Had these past few weeks with my father all been an act? I didn't know who my mum was any more.

She stood facing me with her back to the door. 'You're scared your precious father will find out I've been a bad girl, is that it? Well, I think he should know.'

I got to my feet, terrified. 'You can't do that,' I pleaded. 'He's been through enough.'

'He's been through enough! I'll tell your father what I bleedin' well want. He needs to know how useless he is. I'll tell him everything.'

At that moment the back door slowly opened. My father stood motionless, staring at his wife, at this woman he didn't know, in disgust and disbelief. He leant forward, picked up his keys from the shelf and turned to go. In the doorway, he looked back at my mother now slumped silently in her chair by the range.

'I don't need telling,' he said. 'I heard it all.'

From that day on we lived separate lives. My dad made the front parlour into his bedroom and Mum led her own life.

Chapter Eight

A year on from that day, in September 1947, we had food on the table. We had clothes. We could pay the rent. But we didn't have a family.

My dad still worked at the tannery. He hated it. Soon after my mum's outburst he started going to the pub straight after work. Often I'd hear him come in late at night. Sometimes he'd fall through the door and lie at the bottom of the stairs in a drunken stupor. I had to get up and get him into his room so Mum wouldn't find him and go mad.

One night she was entertaining in the kitchen. Mr Marston, one of her regulars, who owned the furniture shop, had called round. They were having a few drinks.

'You go to bed now, Dolly. Me and Mr

Marston have things to discuss.' My mum turned to him with a sly smile. He was sitting by the range in her chair and he looked at me smugly.

She ushered me out and shut the door behind me. I stood by the door for a minute to listen. I just heard a giggle and the chair moving. That's all I wanted to hear.

I went upstairs to my bedroom. It was the only place I felt I was safe – I was in my own little world. I lay in bed listening to my mum's laughter. I tried to cover my ears to block out the sounds. Suddenly, I heard the front door open and my dad stumbled in. He was swearing so loudly that the next-door neighbours were shouting back.

I realized Dad had gone to the kitchen. I jumped up and raced to the top of the stairs. I heard my mum screaming at him and the sound of pans being thrown. He was calling her every name under the sun. The next thing I saw, as I peered through the banisters, was Mr Marston being lifted up by his shirt front as Dad dragged him into the hall. He had him suspended off the ground. Mr Marston's brown trousers were dangling round his ankles. He was dribbling, almost foaming at the mouth, while protesting his innocence. Mum was behind Dad, trying to stop him. She was punching him and grabbing at his arm to pull him away. At the same time she was desperately trying to pull her dress back on.

Dad almost carried Mr Marston to the front door. He opened the door, held Mr Marston at arm's length and then took one almighty sock at his jaw. Mr Marston went flying onto the cobbles.

I'd never seen my dad look so furious. 'Now bugger off!' he shouted. 'You won't get anything more here.' He slammed the door.

I ran into my room, threw myself on the bed and laughed and laughed till my stomach ached. I had the best night's sleep ever.

The following days blurred into one as my parents drank, shouted and screamed at each other.

I loved my father. My mum I felt sorry for. She was damaged. The war had left scars on all of us. But somehow I knew that Mum was a desperate woman, seeking something to fill the emptiness inside her. Men and drink seemed to be the only things that could blot out the reality of her life.

One night I was lying in bed waiting to see which one of them would come home first. At about eleven o'clock the front door opened and Mum came in. I could smell the familiar mixture of scent and fags. She stumbled through the door, falling but laughing.

I went down to her, knowing that if I didn't persuade her to go to bed she'd end up sleeping on the floor.

'Doll,' she giggled, 'come here.' She sat on the stone floor. 'I've got a secret.' She pulled me down to sit with her. 'Shh,' she said, putting her finger to my lips. 'The liner's gone to America without us. No more dreams, Doll, no yellow dress for you, no dancing for me.'

We sat together on the cold stone floor and she cried a child's juddering cry. I stroked her hair, held her in my arms and quietly sang:

> *'The big ship sails on the ally-ally-oh,*
> *The ally-ally-oh, the ally-ally-oh.*
> *The big ship sails on the ally-ally-oh,*
> *On the last day of September.'*

Chapter Nine

I was nearly seventeen. I had a drunken prostitute for a mother and a worn-out, battered man for a father. A lot of men had come back from the war in a bad mental state. 'Hurting head,' my dad called it. Sometimes I'd see him sitting and holding his head as if it was about to explode.

'It's all right, princess,' he'd say, smiling at me. 'Just trying to stop the voices.'

I didn't understand that he could hear things: the men, the screams, the sound of dying.

He had night terrors. His room was underneath mine and I'd be woken in the night by his cries. It would start with a mumble and then get louder and louder.

The first time I heard it, I thought he was having another row with Mum. Now I was used to the sound. Mum just ignored it. When it first happened she went into the parlour to find out what all the noise was about. A couple of minutes later she started screaming. I ran downstairs and, as I reached the bottom, she staggered out of the room.

'Bloody idiot's just tried to strangle me!' she told me, rubbing her neck with her hands. 'Bloody lunatic!' She shouted at the closed door. 'You want locking up, you do.'

By this time my dad knew all there was to know about what had happened during his years away. Mum didn't bother to hide anything. She had a job at the local pub – the Bull – in the next street. The landlord was the same Mr Jackson who'd come to our house that time.

Sometimes, when I wanted to see where my mother was, I walked round there at night. Just to see she was all right. One night I peeped through the windows, making sure no one could see me. There she was, standing at the piano, while old Ronnie played. Her blouse was undone to show off her cleavage. Her hair was falling all over her face. She had a drink in one hand and she was singing.

There were men all over her. They came up behind her, kissing her neck, their hands everywhere.

I watched them, slavering like dogs, egging each other on. As I was about to go, sickened by the whole spectacle, the noise suddenly rose. I wondered if there was a fight about to break out. I turned back to the window. My mum was standing in the middle of the floor. The men were like savages – swearing and laughing – pushing a young boy, about my age, into the circle they had formed. With one more shove he landed in the open arms of my mum.

It was Stanley Armitage, the undertaker's son.

I didn't know Stanley well, only from school, and as a little kid. He was a shy boy I really liked. He was tall with large dark eyes, but he was far too thin and always had a worried expression. He had always been kind to me and I'd always felt sorry for him. We all knew his father beat him.

The only time I had really spoken to him was at the recreation ground one day. We were about ten or eleven and he had been sitting on the swing, on his own as usual. I had gone over to him. He'd said nothing, but I saw the bruises on his arms and neck which I'd noticed earlier at school. I didn't know what to say.

'One day he'll be in one of them coffins,' he said with a solemn look. 'Then I can bury him and leave here for good.' He looked straight at me and I saw a tear roll down his face. Then he half smiled, touched my hair and ran away.

Now he was being thrown to the lions in the pub and I didn't know what to do.

I watched in horror as he struggled to get away from my mum, but she grabbed his hand and shoved it down her blouse. The men went wild, like a lynch mob. They were pushing Stanley, shouting, 'Nancy boy.' My mum tried to kiss him, but he managed to hold her off. Then two men grabbed his head while she slobbered all over him. At the bar I saw Stanley's father laughing along with the others.

I felt sick. Sick and angry. If my mum wanted to shame herself, then who was to stop her? But to pick on someone like Stanley, that was just unfair. I realized that, watching this spectacle, any sympathy I'd had for my mother had disappeared. She'd chosen to be like this; there was nothing I could do to help her.

Meanwhile, Stanley had fallen to the floor and Mum was screaming with laughter. The men were beside themselves and were grabbing at her as if she was a piece of meat. She was loving it. In the mayhem, Stanley managed to push his way through the crowd. He fell out of the door of the pub on to the cobbles at my feet. He sat very still for a moment, then looked up and saw me. He flushed red. The look of shame on his face was terrible. I couldn't speak. He stood up and walked very deliberately away down the street in the cold night air.

I watched him for a minute and felt such pain. I took one last look through the window. Mum was dancing on her own in the middle of the floor, but the men were losing interest in her. The room started to clear.

I saw a man sitting at the bar with his head on the counter. As I stared at this lone, drunken figure, he lifted his head and tried to get off the stool. He stumbled and, as he reached to steady himself, he turned in my direction. It was my dad. He missed his footing and landed on his knees.

I stared at him with tears in my eyes. He had always seemed so strong to me. Now he was weak and pathetic, a pitiful shadow of the man he had once been.

I knew now that the only person I could depend on was me. I turned and walked home slowly. Alone.

Chapter Ten

The next morning I was out early, to avoid being drawn into a battle.

Although our standard of living had improved when my dad first got his job at the tannery, most of his money was now being spent on alcohol rather than on essentials. Luckily I still had the washing rounds I had made my own, so I could earn and save some money. But I couldn't afford new clothes. And so it was that I was still walking around in the same grey dress I'd had for years. It had been a hand-me-down from my mum.

If there was ever any spare cash for new clothes, my mother was always the one to have them. I'd get her cast-offs. Once my dress had been red and vibrant. Now it was like a washed-out rag. She'd also given me an old coat. Whereas my mum was tall and full-bodied, I was quite slim and petite. So her old clothes hung on me. I looked like the scarecrow that stood in the fields near the recreation ground.

I was on my way to deliver some washing. Halfway down my street I noticed five girls had started to follow me. One I knew: Susan Hardcourt.

When I was still at school, she had been the person to avoid because she was a bully. She always had new leather shoes, white socks, clean clothes. Although she could only have been about ten years old then, she also had enviable bosoms. At the time I had none, and had no idea when, or if, they would grow. She recommended girls to rub mustard on their chests, but it never worked for me. She would go in the bike sheds and let the boys have a look for a ha'penny, a fumble for a penny.

She took every opportunity to call me names. So when I saw her behind me with her friends that morning, I knew there would be trouble. I tried to ignore them but they started to run in front of me, then stop suddenly so they bumped into me. I felt a sudden hard push from behind. They surrounded me, shoving me up against a wall. I didn't even try to escape. I felt a bit like an antelope just before it's attacked by a lion. I accepted the inevitable; I was submissive, pathetic.

Susan started prodding me with her finger and the others joined in. She picked out a piece of clean laundry and threw it on the pavement. I stood numbly as they undid all my work, throwing the washing into the road, tearing at it and jumping on it. I didn't react, which was not what she wanted. The other girls were now in a frenzy, trying to destroy every sheet, shirt and pair of knickers they could. Susan walked over to me slowly.

'Look at me, dummy.'

I refused.

'Look at me, you dirty, filthy, dumb Dolly.' She turned back to her friends, who had gathered round to watch the show. 'Look, girls,' she drawled, 'Dolly's like Cinderella – all dressed in rags.' They laughed like a pack of hyenas.

Still I did nothing.

'Only Dolly will never get a Prince Charming,' Susan taunted me. 'Not unless her whore of a mother casts off her men like she does her clothes.'

I kept my head down, knowing that sooner or later they'd get bored and leave me alone. But Susan was getting meaner.

'If Dolly's so keen on washing everyone else's clothes, maybe we should give her rags a good scrub. Let's give dirty Dolly a wash, shall we?' There were big cheers from the mob. 'Strip her,' she screamed.

They started to tear at my clothes. Suddenly Susan's face was right next to mine.

'No Prince Charming to the rescue,' she spat at me. 'You're pathetic, Dolly dummy. Just like your dad. Your mother sleeps around and he just sleeps. He's a no-good waster. A drunk. A silly old sod. He'd be better off dead.'

That did it. Suddenly, like a mighty lion, I rose up from the ground and lashed out at my tormentors. I grabbed hold of Susan. She stood there with her mouth open, caught by surprise. I managed to get a couple of really good slaps in before her mates pulled me off her.

There was screaming and swearing.

Then there was a white heat and a blackness. I woke to find myself being cradled in Stanley Armitage's arms. I tried to jump up, but my head was pounding. I fell back into his embrace.

''S all right. You had a right nasty blow from that cow, Susan,' he said. 'Bloody cowards – they went running off when I came over. Mind, she came off worse.' He laughed. 'You gave her a hell of a smack. Bet she never bothers you again.'

We both sat on the pavement, surrounded by dirty washing. I was cut and bruised but remembered the look of shock on Susan's face when I grabbed her. I started to laugh.

'We're a couple of odd ones, you and me, Stanley. Just look at us.'

He grinned. 'I hope no one thinks I was trying to steal your knickers,' he said, gesturing at the spilled laundry. 'I'd get a reputation.'

We both started laughing. If anyone had seen us lying among all that washing and laughing so hard we couldn't breathe, they'd have locked us up.

I ached. But I didn't care. For the first time in a long time, I felt secure.

From that day on Stanley Armitage was part of my life. For richer or poorer, in sickness and in health, till death . . .

Chapter Eleven

I stayed away from home as much as possible. Mum carried on working at the pub, Dad at the tannery – when he was sober.

I continued to take in as much washing as I could, helped pay the bills, cleaned the house and always had food in the larder to make sure we all had something to eat.

An ominous calm had fallen over the house since that night at the pub; it was worrying. I did my best to ignore the tension and keep out of the way.

Me and Stanley went for walks in Draycott Park on the other side of the recreation ground. We knew we wouldn't be seen, because few people went near the park. Rumour had it that some German soldiers were hiding there. As it was three years since the end of the war, we thought if they were there, they would either be dead from hunger or so glad to see us that they wouldn't harm us.

It was raining and we were sitting under the big oak tree. Stanley started to tell me how much he had loved his mother, and how he believed his father had driven her to her death.

'She loved life,' he said. 'She wanted to read and learn. Maybe even go on to be a teacher or something like that.' His face drained of colour at the obviously painful memories. 'Dad beat it out of her. He told her she was good for nothing, only useful for cleaning and cooking and the like. I'd hear them at night. She'd beg him to stop. I used to lie in bed, waiting for the end. I vowed when I was older I'd kill him.'

'Then they'd take you away,' I said.

I stroked his hands. They were strong and warm. He touched my lips with his fingers, parting them slightly. I felt an incredible sensation tingle through my body. He stared into my eyes and slowly leant down until his lips touched mine. I knew there and then we would always be one. When he pulled away and I looked at him, he smiled such a sweet smile. I never wanted this moment to end.

*

It was 1949. I was eighteen; Stanley was nineteen. No one knew about us. The thought of his father, or my mother, finding out worried both of us. So we were very careful. But we made lots of plans.

Stanley had very bad days with his father, as I did with my mum. He still hated his father, but because we had our secret life it helped to soothe the situation.

We shared the occasional kiss, but didn't even talk about sex. I just knew it had to be something foul and disgusting. I had seen my mum being man-handled in the pub. I had heard the animal-like noises coming from my mum's room when she 'entertained'. Stanley's experiences had been just as bad. He had heard his father hurt his mother, night after night. If that is what sex amounted to, then we wanted nothing to do with it.

Once, when we were sitting under our tree, Stanley reached over to swat away a bee. In doing so, he accidentally stroked the back of his hand over my breasts. We both froze.

'Sorry,' he whispered.

'Yes,' I said.

'Yes?'

'No, I mean.'

'No?'

We both got a fit of giggles and lay laughing till we cried. I didn't dislike his touch, but I never told Stanley that.

At home the house was still my responsibility. I only went into my mum's room when I knew she was out. I very rarely went near my father's. The smell of the tannery on his clothes made me feel sick, especially in warm weather. Mum was right. It did bring a feeling of death into the house.

My one wish was to escape: to leave with Stanley and never look back. I knew he felt the same way.

Chapter Twelve

It was Christmas. We didn't celebrate it as a family now. There was no money for presents anyway, and my parents drank more than usual and would then argue and fight. So it was a time I really dreaded. But this year I had hope. This year there was me and Stanley.

It was Christmas Eve. I had worked so hard all day to get all my washing done early. My hands were like wrinkled old gloves, but I didn't care if it meant I could see Stanley that evening. He did the same. He didn't fall out with his father and kept his temper when the large fat hand was lifted and brought down on his back. So Christmas Eve was free.

Mum was in her room getting ready for work at the pub. Dad was still at the tannery, but he would probably be going out with his workmates straight afterwards to celebrate the coming Christmas holiday.

It was four o'clock; I was still in the kitchen just finishing the last of my washing. I heard Mum's bedroom door open and down the stairs she came. I could hear her high heels clip-clopping on the boards. She stopped at the bottom.

'Dolly?' she shouted.

I stayed quiet and hoped she'd leave. She was so out of control these days that anything could happen, and I didn't want to risk losing my evening with Stanley.

'Dolly, come here. If I have to come into that kitchen, you'll get such a slap. Get yourself out here now.'

I knew I had to go. I opened the door slowly, hoping she would be quick with whatever it was she wanted.

'There you are,' she said. 'Do my skirt up.'

Gone were the days of seeing her in a red silk frock with her hair taken up to the side and gently falling over her face. Now it was tight skirts and low-cut blouses with everything hanging out. I could hardly fasten the zip, her skirt was so tight. She swung round and stood looking at me critically.

'You don't like me dressing like this, do you?' I could smell alcohol on her breath.

I said nothing and she gave a bitter laugh and strutted towards the front door.

I thought the moment of danger was over and made a crucial mistake. I sighed.

She placed her hand on the door knob, then paused. There was a silence and then she turned and walked back towards me.

'Sighing in disappointment at your old slapper of a mother, are you? Don't you dare stand there judging me, you little bitch.' She moved closer. 'I know about you and your dirty boyfriend,' she hissed.

I went cold and stared at her.

'Don't play the innocent with me. I know where you've been. In the woods? Well, well, looks like you are your mother's daughter after all.'

She laughed so hard that she couldn't catch her breath.

I couldn't bear to have everything I had with Stanley turned into something grubby by her. I felt a sick burning feeling in my stomach and a red mist rose over my eyes. I grabbed her hair and pulled it so hard it made her stumble. I quickly let go, terrified at what I'd just done.

As she struggled to right herself she managed to lash out at me, cutting my cheek with the gaudy dress ring she always wore. I fell back against the wall. Blood was welling from my scratched face. I ran into the kitchen and dabbed at the cut with a damp cloth, knowing that it would probably leave a scar. A scar would be my mum's legacy to me. I didn't cry; I was too angry. I had so wanted this evening to be special for Stanley and me.

I felt her looming in the kitchen door.

'You have to make a drama out of it, don't you? Oh, poor little Dolly! What will the boyfriend think now?'

I glared at her.

'And don't go running to your father; he won't care.' A strange weakness in her voice struck me. 'He's too drunk to care about anyone. Even his precious little princess won't separate him from his bottle.' Slurring her words, she carried on, 'You think you're so different, don't you? I was like you once. I had my dreams. I was in love. I would have done so much if you hadn't come along. I'd have got rid of you if I could, but your bloody father put a stop to that.'

I'd heard all this before and I knew it was best to keep quiet until she was done, but my silence angered her. She started to slam about the kitchen, pushing the table, kicking the chairs. 'Look at me. Look at me!' she screamed.

I turned slowly from the sink holding a bloody cloth to my cheek and stared at her. A pathetic, small, lifeless creature stared back. There was silence as we looked at each other properly for the first time in years. There was nothing left of the mother I'd once known. Instead there was a broken woman with all her dreams crushed. And me? I was a worn-out eighteen-year-old girl trying to hold together the remnants of a family that no longer existed.

Suddenly I felt a sense of freedom. There and then I decided to leave home. There was nothing left for me here. I had no idea how I could get away, what I would do, where I would go. But I knew that Stanley and I could have some happiness together. Certainly more than we had at the moment, trapped with our vile parents.

Mum and I stood in that frozen position for a few minutes. Neither of us wanted to be the first to move.

As if reading my mind, she came up close and said very deliberately, 'You can't go anywhere, missy. You have work to do.' Then she reached out to touch my face. I turned my head away. Lowering her voice, she said, 'Think on, you'll end up just like me. Tied down. A prisoner. See how it feels for the next twenty years. Look at me, Doll.' She took hold of my face. I winced with pain but made no sound. 'Look at me. Look at your old mum, Doll. You're looking at yourself.'

I raised my eyes to hers. 'My mum disappeared years ago,' I said quietly. 'She doesn't exist any more. I am not my mother's daughter.'

I held my breath, waiting for a smack across my poor bloody cheek. She said nothing. Letting go of my face, she backed away, as though I was the one who had slapped her. She looked at me so piercingly I had to turn away. There was silence. Then the front door slammed and she was gone.

Chapter Thirteen

My determination to leave now was absolute. I went upstairs and tried to tidy myself up. The bleeding had stopped.

After my encounter with Susan, I had taken to stealing clothes from Mum's room. She never noticed anything missing.

So dressed all in blue, my stolen shoes slightly too big, but packed with paper to make them fit, I grabbed my mother's best coat and started down the stairs.

At that moment I heard the front door open. I was terrified she'd come back. I listened carefully. The parlour door creaked. It was Dad.

I flew down the stairs, stopped outside his door for a second, then pushed it open.

'Dad?'

It was dark in the front room. He never opened the heavy green curtains.

'Dad?'

A shadowy figure was slumped on the settee which doubled as his bed. I walked into the gloomy, smelly room. A heavy odour of the tannery lay in the air.

'Princess?' he spoke softly, his voice filled with such gentle love it made me want to cry. 'Come here, princess.'

I threw myself on the sofa beside him. I hugged him like a small child and sobbed so hard it took his breath away.

'No, no, no, little girl. What's this all about?' He held me so tight, then lifted my chin. 'What would upset my princess so much?' He stopped as he saw my cut cheek.

I'd forgotten my face. He reached over and switched on the lamp. I tried to cover the cut with my hand.

'Who did this?' he asked so quietly, sounding so kind.

I shook my head.

'You have to tell me, princess,' he said sternly.

'I can't.'

'Was it this boy your mum says you've met?'

I was so stunned he should know about

Stanley, I couldn't say anything.

'What's his name? Stanley Armitage, isn't it?'

I stared at him miserably. I'd wanted for so long to be able to talk to my dad about Stanley. To be able to tell him how much I cared for him. How I'd finally found someone who loved me and wanted to look after me. But what would Dad think? Would he think I was like my mum as well?

I nodded carefully.

He jumped up. 'I know who that kid is. The little bastard! I'll sort him out.'

'NO,' I shouted, realizing that Dad thought Stanley had done this to me.

I'd never seen him so furious. 'Don't you start defending the little shit now. He's going to get what's coming to him.'

He dragged his coat from the back of the chair.

'I told you not to mess with boys.'

I grabbed at his arm, pleading with him to listen to me. But he'd made his mind up. He believed Stanley had done it, and that was that.

He walked towards the door but I stood in front of him, refusing to let him leave. 'It wasn't him, Dad. He wouldn't hurt me. He'd always try to protect me, but this time he couldn't.' I stopped. I didn't know how to carry on.

'Couldn't? Why couldn't he? What's wrong with him that he couldn't? Is he soft?'

I just looked down. How could I tell him that Mum had done this to me?

He pushed past me and picked up the stick he always took with him when he went out for a walk.

'That little shit is going to pay for this.'

I ran over to him and tried to grab the stick. 'Don't! Please, you're wrong! He didn't touch me.'

As we fought, he pushed me. 'Don't defend the bastard. Don't lower yourself to your lying mother's level.' He turned again towards the door.

With that I screamed, 'It was her!' I was nearly choking through my tears. 'It was Mum. She did this. She's the one who hit me.'

I collapsed on the floor in a heap, sobbing till my heart hurt.

He leant down and pulled me to my feet.

'Shh, shh, no more tears, princess. I'll take care of everything now.'

He seemed so calm. He lifted me up and gently lowered me on to the settee. He took off my shoes, then covered me with his heavy winter coat and kissed the top of my head.

'Sleep, princess.'

His big, rough hands gently soothed my forehead as if willing me into sleep. I could feel myself drifting away as if everything was floating. I could hardly hear Dad. I tried to open my eyes but they were too heavy. His voice sounded so far away. I tried to speak, to stop him from going anywhere. I just wanted him to stay with me, but my mouth wouldn't move.

He hugged me tightly. I felt such love flow towards me from him. I had never felt such love before.

'I love you, Dad,' I heard myself say.

There was the sound of a stifled sob. 'I love you too, princess.'

Then there was stillness, peace.

Chapter Fourteen

My eyes slowly opened. I could see my breath in the cold air. My face hurt and felt stiff and bruised. I put my hand up to touch my cheek. It was encrusted with dried blood.

The room was freezing. I threw off my dad's coat and as I did so I suddenly gagged on the pungent smell of death. My dad's room reeked of the tannery. The stench was always present. Another wave of dead cow smell wafted over me and I dry-heaved.

I could hear my mum's voice in my head. 'That bloody father of yours with that tannery. It's enough to make us all sick.'

I looked at the clock; it was very late. I must have been asleep for a long time. I wrapped my dad's coat back round me. I was shivering, not just from cold but from the memory of what I'd said, which was flooding back. After years of keeping quiet, had I really finally told him about Mum? Had he believed me? Where had he gone?

I couldn't stay in that room any longer. I had to do something.

The front door opened. I wondered whether it was my father. I stayed as still as I could.

There was a clatter from the hallway. 'Bloody shoes,' I heard Mum say as she obviously tripped over them.

There was a gravelly laugh from a strange man. 'Come 'ere, you daft old bag.'

It was a voice I didn't recognize.

There was a muffled giggle from Mum. 'Don't start that in the hallway, you randy sod. Get off.' There was the sound of a thump.

The strange man cursed and raised his voice. 'You stupid bitch! I nearly smacked my head on that door.' I could hear scuffles, a slap, and a yell.

My mum's voice rang out crossly. 'Don't you hit me, you bastard.'

'Come 'ere! I'll do what I want. I'm paying enough for it,' the voice said, slurring the words.

Then there was a ripping sound. Another

fumble. A giggle from Mum. 'Let's go upstairs to my room where we can be comfy.'

With that I heard them stumble up the stairs and my mum's door banged shut.

I went slowly to the door, opened it and looked out. I could hear laughter and grunting from upstairs. I felt sick. I rushed out of the room, opened the front door and ran. It didn't matter that I had no shoes on. I just needed to get away from that decaying house as quickly as possible. I didn't stop running until I reached the house where Stanley lived with his father.

I must have looked a sight. I still had on my mum's old blue serge dress. I had no shoes, a cut and bloodied face, and was as white as a sheet.

I stood across the road from the house staring at the sign: Armitage Funeral Directors. I was trying to gather up the nerve to go in. I'd always liked the undertaker's sign. I'd found out that Stanley had come up with the line that was underneath: 'For everyone you hold dear – let their sun set here (we measure free of charge).'

For some reason that really made me smile

now, then I started to laugh out loud. I had visions of that horrible little man in my house measuring my mum on the kitchen table, and her yelling at him for not doing it right. 'Bloody silly little man! It's from the top of my head to my toes. Watch me hair, I've just had it done!'

I stood there crying and laughing, leaning against the wall. I felt helpless. I couldn't move. My face had started to bleed again. The laughing had opened the wound. I felt a hand under my arm. I struggled and punched out, not quite knowing where I was.

'It's all right; it's me. It's all right; you're safe now.' Stanley pulled me to him and cuddled me. He put his arm round my shoulders and guided me round the back of the funeral parlour and up the stairs.

'Dad's out,' Stanley explained. 'So let's get you up to my room. We'll have to be quiet, but you're staying with me.'

He never asked me what I was doing there, or why I was in such a state. He didn't need to ask who had hit me. He knew me well enough to know the answer. We went up to his attic bedroom. Because the back stairs were steep and narrow, Stanley's father never went up there. It was Stanley's, and now my refuge. It was quite dark but strangely warm. There was a single bed in the corner, a small gas fire, two armchairs and a rag rug. Stanley told me that his grandma had made it out of some old coats belonging to his grandfather.

He sat me down in one of the chairs and lit the fire. It gave off a warm glow, soothing my aching bones. I sat there for some time, half asleep. Nothing was said.

Some time later, Stanley stood me up and walked me over to the bed. He stroked my hair and gently kissed my face. I looked at him, not knowing what he was going to do. He slowly undid the buttons on my dress, letting it fall to the floor. As if I was a child he lifted my feet one by one out of the dress. He kissed the back of my neck. I stood waiting as he pulled the covers back and lowered me on to the bed. He covered me over, and then leant down, kissed me again, and said, 'Sleep well, princess.'

Chapter Fifteen

My mum's face was next to mine. Her hot stinking breath flowed over me – a stale smell of alcohol and cigarettes. 'You dirty little bitch. Here with your fancy man.' Her red lips were like a gash in her face. Her teeth were yellowed and stained with lipstick. 'Where is he, then, eh? Gone now, hasn't he? I told him what you really were. Just like me, your mother's daughter, that's what you are! What would he want with a little slut like you?'

I started to hit her, thump her. I wanted to smash her foul face to stop the vile words coming from her. I was screaming at her. I sobbed, begged, pleaded with her to bring him back and tell him it was a lie. 'I hate you! Leave Stanley alone. Leave me alone!'

I could hear her taunting me: 'Dolly, Dolly.' I punched and punched.

'Dolly, stop. It's all right. Stop. You're mother's not here; you're with me; you're safe.'

Stanley laid me back on the pillow. There was no one else in the room and I realized with relief that I had been dreaming. Sweat was pouring from me. I felt as though I was burning up. He put a cold flannel on my forehead. I sobbed and sobbed while he rocked me in his arms. He held me for what seemed like for ever. I never wanted him to let me go.

In the soft morning light of his room, I could see the red glow of the fire over his shoulder and feel the warmth of his arms. His smell was my smell and I wanted it with me always. It had just been a nightmare, I knew that. But the nightmare that was my life still existed. My mother still existed. Would I never be free of her? Stanley tucked me in and kissed my nose. I was loved. Sleep came.

I drifted in and out of consciousness most of Christmas morning. But I was always aware of Stanley in the room. He changed the flannel on my forehead every now and then. At one point he lifted me up off the pillow and supported me while feeding me some soup.

But my tiredness was so powerful I gave in to it and floated away again.

In my dreams I saw my father. He was walking through a park. I was walking behind him but every time I nearly caught up with him, he walked a bit faster. I tried to call to him, to tell him to wait for me, but he didn't seem to hear me. He had a threadbare grey suit on, and every time there was a gust of wind part of the suit ripped. Bits of it were flying everywhere. I tried to catch them but, as I reached up to grab a piece, it turned to blood which dripped down my arm. I screamed at him to stop, but he had started running. I ran after him but my feet were too heavy and my legs wouldn't work properly. Although I was making an immense effort, I wasn't moving.

Then he stopped and just stood there in his blood-stained rags. He turned to look at me. His face was cut and scarred. 'Don't go back, princess,' he said. Then a gust of wind came and blew dust and leaves in swirling patterns so I couldn't see anything. When the wind died down, he had gone. I called out to him but there was a hand over my mouth. I struggled, trying to pull the hand away.

'Shh, Dolly. Shh, my dad's downstairs. We don't want him knowing you're here.' I was suddenly aware where I was and that Stanley was trying to protect me. The dream was over, but I knew then something was wrong at home and I had to go back.

'How long have I been asleep?' I asked. I sat up and watched as he quietly moved round the room.

'You slept all through last night and now it's the afternoon of Christmas Day,' he said, smiling. He made me a sandwich and a cup of tea, something no one had done for me for years. 'I'm going down to see my dad. We haven't got any work on today as it's Christmas,' he said, 'so I'll just see what he's going to do. He'll probably go to the pub, then we can talk.' As he made for the door, he turned to look at me. 'There's just you and me now; we'll make it.' He gave me a smile so warm that, for a moment, I wanted time to stand still.

After he'd gone I strained to hear what was happening. I heard raised voices; I couldn't understand what they were saying but it sounded as though it was a bad row. I made out a few words: 'lazy' and 'good for nothing' along with 'no son of mine' and 'useless'. All the things Stanley had told me his father said about him. Stanley didn't shout back, never said a word. At that moment, just as he was my salvation so was I his. He couldn't have cared less what his father thought of him. He knew what I thought, and I'm sure all he wanted was for his father to go out so we could be together.

The door downstairs slammed. I could hear his father's boots striking the cobbles outside the funeral parlour and marching away down the road. There was more movement downstairs as Stanley locked the front doors to the funeral parlour.

It was getting dark by the time he came back up into the room. And before I could say anything, he'd already started to speak: 'You can't go back home tonight, Dolly. I know what you're thinking, but I think you should stay here with me. Get your strength back, and tomorrow we will sort it all out together. Start as we mean to go on.'

But I was worried. 'I've never left them alone before,' I explained. 'My mum's got a filthy temper and I've never seen my dad so angry as when he found out it was Mum who hit me. I just don't know what will happen if the two of them start on one another.'

As I was speaking I had been trying to get out of bed, but I felt so weak that I realized Stanley was right. He came over to the bed and sat beside me.

'You are staying here. You are my responsibility now. What can't wait till tomorrow? Let them deal with their own mess for a change. Whatever happens, we'll sort it out in the morning.'

He was so strong, so determined. He'd grown into a man, seemingly overnight. I knew he wouldn't let me go and I thanked God for it. 'Your father, when will he be back?'

'He's staying with his fancy bit tonight. Mrs Dewsbury, the drayman's widow. He won't be back until the morning now.' I lay back in Stanley's bed and felt a relief that, for tonight at least, I could sleep without fear of being woken by the drunken activities of my parents.

I felt joy and such hope for the future that I had never dared to dream of before.

Chapter Sixteen

Christmas night was one of wonderment for me and Stanley. We were in our own little world in that little room. Just the two of us. We were warm, there was no fear, and we both felt drunk on laughter and freedom. For the first time there was no one telling us how useless and unwanted we were. We wanted each other, and that was enough.

We talked about everything, as we always did, but this time things had changed. Now we were talking of a future we knew we could have if we just had the courage to reach out and grab it. We knew, from that night on, we would be together. We had everything we wanted and no one could touch us.

I sat and watched Stanley clear up. He collected the dirty crockery and took it downstairs to the kitchen and tidied the room up. I'd never seen a man perform any of those sorts of tasks before.

Then he came over to me and sat next to me on the bed.

I looked into his eyes. 'Do you know how much I love you?' I asked him with a smile.

He looked down with a blush staining his cheeks.

I stroked his hair, lifted his face with my fingers and traced the outline of his lips with my fingertip.

He gently opened his mouth and kissed my fingers. Then turned my hand over and kissed my palm. He took my face in both his hands and kissed my lips. I could feel a slow warmth burning and growing in me.

'I love you so much. I always have,' he whispered.

He lay down next to me. Both of us were scared and without any experience. We fumbled and stopped and laughed. But because we loved each other it seemed the most natural thing in the world. I managed to take his shirt off at long last, and I realized he was no longer the thin young boy I had once known, but a man. A man I wanted to be held and loved by.

It was terrifying for both of us. But it felt right and it felt as though everything in our lives had been leading up to this moment. It seemed like the right time.

His body was strong and his hands were tender and loving. When he caressed my body, the sensation was so electric that I shuddered with joy. He was so careful and gentle that when we finally came together the sensation was overwhelming. The heat of that moment is something I will never forget. As I held his body tight I knew this had given us the strength to face the world and anything life could throw at us.

Chapter Seventeen

We had talked our plans through. We had decided to tell my parents first. Then come back and face Mr Armitage. We got up and left Stanley's room early, afraid of bumping into his dad too soon. We had to do this our way.

We hurried down Century Road. We were holding hands and felt completely determined and sure of our course. We walked past the recreation ground where we'd sat all that time ago, when Stanley first touched my hair and I saw such pain in his eyes. Then on past the pub where my mum had grabbed and humiliated him, with his father watching, jeering and baying along with all the other men.

We turned into my street and I stopped. The rush of adrenalin was making me shake. I was freezing yet burning inside and I suddenly couldn't move.

I stared at our house. The stone steps were grubby through lack of care. The net curtains were hanging crookedly and looking dirty. I thought sadly of how my life had been when I was a little girl before the war. How well my mother had kept the house and how happy we had all been.

Stanley gave my arm a little shake. 'Don't be afraid, Dolly. We've agreed, haven't we?' He took my hands in his. 'You and me, Doll. That's all we need.'

'I don't know, I can't think,' I whispered.

He hugged me tightly for a second. 'We have to face them,' he said. He looked down at me and kissed me gently on the forehead. 'And we'll face them together. I won't let anyone hurt you. Let's go.'

We walked across the road and up to the house.

The front door was slightly open. I pushed it and, as it swung back, I noticed dark stains on the floor. With a gasp, I realized the stains were blood and I took a step back, knocking into Stanley, who was right behind me. A feeling of dread welled up in both of us.

Stanley pushed past me and slowly stepped

inside. I followed him. The hallway was dark and silent. The door to my dad's room was wide open. I could smell the faint, metallic smell of blood. I couldn't catch my breath; my chest felt tight. We moved cautiously down the hall. Stanley shoved me back into the shadows as he opened the kitchen door. He walked into the room; I could just see past him. It was gloomy but there was a little light filtering in through a small uncurtained window.

Suddenly a shadowy figure rushed past me from the parlour. It was screaming and waving a knife. Before I could move, or do anything, it was threatening Stanley with the knife. I shouted a warning, and he turned and stumbled backwards. I was almost blinded by the tears cascading down my cheeks. Stanley slipped and fell on the floor. He raised his arms trying to protect himself from the waving knife.

I shouted again and the figure turned and glared at me. It was my mother. Rage had twisted her features, her eyes were bloodshot and I could smell booze coming off her in waves. She looked completely out of control.

She stared at me for a moment. Then Stanley started to get up and she swung back towards him.

'Mum, no! Please no!' I called to her, trying desperately to bring her back to her senses. She ignored me and slashed at Stanley. He fell to the floor again just in time to avoid the knife, but she must have nicked his wrist because blood started to run down his arm. He was pinned against the table legs and the kitchen sink and unable to move.

I felt around on the shelves trying to find something, anything, to throw at her, or hit her with, anything to distract her.

She stood above Stanley shouting, 'You won't take her. You won't!' She waved the knife high above her head.

I was panic-stricken. I really believed she was going to kill him.

My searching hands grabbed hold of something cold and hard. Grasping it tightly, I hurled the flat iron as hard as I could towards her. It bounced off the side of her head and her body spun round with the force of it, so she was facing me. Her eyes bulged, pleading with me as she tried to reach out to grab me to keep her balance. I went towards her, but she slipped backwards. There was a loud crack as she fell and smacked her head against the grate. Then she was still.

There was silence. The only noise was the ticking of the clock on the mantelpiece.

She was slumped at my feet.

I felt completely numb.

She looked calm, as though she was sleeping, but there was a pool of blood spreading from the back of her head where she'd hit the grate. And she wasn't breathing.

My chest tightened. I fell to my knees and gasped, trying to force some air into my lungs.

Stanley moaned. That woke me out of my stupor.

I crawled over to him. He was staring at me with pain-glazed eyes.

'I need you to stop the bleeding,' I heard him say. 'Tear up some cloth and tie it tightly round my arm. That should do it.'

Yes, I could do that. There were still piles of sheets waiting to be returned to their owners. They had been carefully washed and ironed by me and were stacked on the table. Ironed with the iron I'd just killed my mum with.

I reached over and picked up a sheet belonging to Mrs Dainty, the fat, nasty piece of work who thought we were common. Well, this would teach her. I tore her sheets into long strips. Then I wrapped a long, thin piece tightly round Stanley's wrist several times and tied another piece round his upper arm to try to stop the flow of blood.

I glanced over at the figure on the floor. My mum lay so still. She looked at peace now. No more shouting. I went over to her. It didn't seem right to just leave her lying there all alone. I sat next to her on the floor, pushed her hair from her face, and wiped the blood away with my sleeve.

'It's all right, Mum. Everything will be fine now,' I whispered to her as I held her in my arms. 'I'm not going anywhere. I'm here to look after you.' I rocked her like a baby and softly sang, 'The big ship sails on the ally-ally-oh, the ally-ally-oh, On the last day of September.'

Chapter Eighteen

There was movement all around me. Feet came in and out. There were voices murmuring. Mum and I sat calmly together listening to the noise. I tried to tell them, 'Shh, Mum's sleeping.' But they didn't listen.

'Be quiet! All of you. We are resting, aren't we, Mum?'

Then I felt strong arms lifting me up. I looked down at my mother still lying on the floor. She looked pathetic and lonely. I tried to reach her again but I was held back.

I heard a gentle voice. 'Leave her now, Dolly. Everything will be taken care of.'

The voice was so soft and kind. I did as it said. I could always go back to see if Mum was all right later. She'd probably feel much better after her sleep. She'd want to go out. I could help her with her hair. Pin it up one side, let it all fall down the other side. Just the way she liked it. She'd wear her lovely red dress.

As I was being steered towards the door I turned round. 'Don't forget to come back for me, Mum,' I called. 'We'll go to the port and get on that liner. Sail away like you always said. Blow me a kiss, Mum.'

The next thing I was aware of was that I was sitting in a car wrapped in a blanket, with a hot cup of tea in my hands. A lady I didn't recognize was sitting with me. She had on a blue suit with silver buttons. It looked terribly smart and I wondered if she was from the army.

Then a younger man got in. There was something familiar about his face and I wondered if I'd met him somewhere. He looked as though he'd been in a fight. He had blood on his clothes and his wrist was bandaged. He smiled at me gently and tried to reach for my hand, but I pulled it away. My mum always told me not to talk to strange men.

We drove off in the car and got out at a big, official-looking building. They took me inside and led me to a room. There wasn't much furniture and it was very cold. There was a bed in it, so I lay down on the bed and pulled the covers round me.

The young man drew up a chair beside me.

'Dolly.' I wasn't sure how he knew my name. 'Dolly, it's me, Stanley. Do you know where you are?'

I ignored him, hoping he'd go away.

He stroked my hair.

'I'm here, Dolly. I won't leave you.'

I didn't speak. Who was he? He seemed to know me; I had no idea who he was. I covered my head with the blanket.

Moments later the door opened and I looked out to see another man come in. His clothes were crumpled and dirty. They smelt. It was a smell I'd come across before. Memories of blood started to come to the surface of my mind and I pushed them back down. I didn't want to know.

This new stranger was older than the man who called himself Stanley. But he also had blood all over his clothes and bandages on his arms and a big one wrapped round his chest. I could see the bulk of it underneath his shirt.

He walked over to the bed and fell to his knees. He had tears in his eyes.

I felt as though my heart was going to explode. There was so much emotion in his expression and so much confusion in my head. I just wanted everyone to leave me alone.

'Dolly, what have we done to you?' He looked up at me and sobbed painfully. He took one of my hands in his. His hands were hard and lumpy with calluses. They were stained a ruddy colour and I looked down at my own hands, which seemed to be covered in red as well.

'I'm so sorry, princess. I didn't want you to be part of any of this. I couldn't bear what she'd done to you. I told her to get out, princess, to leave, so we could all get on with our lives. But she wouldn't listen. She said she'd never let you go. Then she went mad, hitting me, and then suddenly she had a knife in her hand. She slashed at me a couple of times with that knife. I just ran out of the door. I didn't know where you were. I wanted to go looking for you, but I had to go and get stitched up. I was bleeding all over the place. When I finally managed to get to the hospital, the doctors called the police. I was unconscious for some time, but when I woke I told them what had happened. I should have stayed at the house in case you came back. I should have made sure she got locked up.'

I listened to the old man as he sobbed out his story. I felt sorry for him. He'd obviously had a very difficult time. But I thought his injuries must have made him very confused, because I had no idea what he was talking about.

Finally the two men were made to leave the room and a young lady talked to me about my mum. I didn't know why she wanted to know about her, but I told her everything. About how Mum liked to go out to the pub, and how all the men really liked her.

She asked me if I got on with my mother. I thought of her red dress swirling, her lovely red hair and the blood. Apart from that my mind was a complete blank.

'Of course, I love my mum,' I told the woman. I explained how Mum was going to take me on a big ship with her one day and we were going to sail to America. 'She promised me a lovely yellow dress with yellow satin shoes.'

The woman nodded and made some notes in a notebook she had. 'Did your mother treat you well?'

Treat me well! I wanted to say yes, but my thoughts started to dance.

'I don't think she really likes me,' I whispered. I rather liked this lady. She smelt clean and her writing was small and neat, so I didn't mind telling her some secrets. 'She didn't want me, you see. I stopped her from doing all the things she wanted to do. She missed out because she had to look after me.' I stopped, feeling guilty. 'Don't tell her I said any of this.'

'Why not?' the lady asked.

'She'll go mad,' I told her, looking fearfully over my shoulder. 'Please, please don't say anything to her.'

The lady looked at me sadly. 'No, of course not. Don't you worry. Would she hurt you if I did?'

I frowned. 'She never really means to,' I explained. 'She just lashes out.'

'Is that how you got that cut on your face? Did she lash out at you and do that?'

I stared at her, not understanding the question.

She gestured to my cheek. I put my hands up to my face and I could feel a cut. It still hurt.

'Did she do that? Did you have to defend yourself from her? How violent was she? Did she beat you?'

There were too many questions all at once. I could see my mum in my mind's eye. She was laughing. She was drinking. She was spinning and spinning in her red dress. She was angry. She was happy. She was falling. Falling so hard and so fast I couldn't catch her. 'Catch it, Doll. Catch it, Doll.'

The room started to spin and everything went black.

I had been drifting in and out of consciousness for what seemed like only a few hours, but I was told that almost two weeks had passed. I'd been screaming for my mum. Singing songs and begging her not to leave me. I don't remember any of it. When I finally woke up and fully regained consciousness, I found myself in a bed. It had high sides like a baby's cot. I looked through the bars on the bed. There was a little teddy bear lying next to me.

Then I heard a familiar voice.

'We have to move you from here, Dolly. I know you don't understand.' A gentle hand took mine and started to stroke it. I closed my eyes and listened to the voice. I daren't open my eyes in case it was a dream. In case he disappeared.

'You've been here for two weeks now, Doll. Your dad and me, we've been here every day. We take it in turns to talk to you, hoping you may remember things.'

He took both of my hands in his and kissed my fingers. It felt good.

'I thought you would remember Draycott Park, all those times we sat under our tree and made plans of leaving and being together?' He stopped. His hands were shaking as they gently put mine back onto the sheet. I heard him blow his nose. 'You remember that Susan Hardcourt, don't you?' His voice was quavering. 'When you smacked her and we sat on that pavement surrounded by all your washing and laughed. You said, "We're odd ones, you and me." Well, we are, Dolly, but we have each other now. Your mum's gone, Dolly. She can't hurt you any more. Your dad's great. We've got to know each other in the last couple of weeks. He nearly belted me at first because of your staying away from home with me. But I went back to the house with him and we sat and talked. He told me all about you and your mum. And then, since you've been in here, you've said a lot more about it all.'

I nearly opened my eyes then. What had I said? I couldn't remember.

'Why did you never explain things to me, Dolly? All the men – Mr Doby, that bloody landlord, Marston. You never said. It must have been really awful.'

He laughed. It's such a familiar laugh. It's a laugh of suffering, of pain, of a shared understanding. I opened my eyes and looked at him. He had his head buried in his hands and he'd started to cry.

'I love you, Dolly. Come back to me. We have all our lives ahead of us now.'

I reached out and took hold of his hand. He looked at me in shock, a slow smile spreading across his face as if he wasn't sure whether I was real or not.

'I love you too, Stanley Armitage,' I said. 'I'm back and you're never losing me again. We have the rest of our lives to spend together.'

Chapter Nineteen

Although I had my memory back, I was still physically and mentally weak. Part of the problem had been an infection I'd got from the cut on my face. For the last two weeks I'd been feverish and unaware of who or where I was. Poor Stanley looked almost as pale and wan as I did. He'd been so worried about me.

They sent me to convalesce at Paisley's cottage hospital, which was a very small and friendly place. Stanley came to see me every day. I still couldn't speak about what had happened that day, and I didn't remember much about it. I kept seeing the occasional flash of red. Or my mother's snarling face. But then there'd be nothing more.

I wondered about my dad. I wanted to know where he had gone. Stanley seemed to think that he felt guilty about not having stopped things earlier, that he couldn't face me. It was probably true, but I needed to see him. Did he blame me for what had happened?

Stanley talked to me every day about life outside the hospital. What we would do and where we would go when I was well enough to leave. He talked always of the future, never of the past. And we never talked about what had happened that day in the kitchen. Or about my mum.

I was getting stronger and stronger. Everyone said how well I was doing, but I still felt half alive, as if something inside me was dead and numb.

One afternoon, while I was sitting on a bench outside waiting for Stanley, I saw a woman in a red dress standing by a tree. It was a bit too far for me to recognize her. I stood up, intrigued. It didn't look like anyone from the hospital. She turned and waved. I looked behind me to see who she could be waving to, but no one was looking that way. I started to walk towards her. The hospital was set at the top of a hill so it was quite steep. I began to run. The woman threw back her head and seemed to be laughing. Then she disappeared round the other side of the tree.

When I reached the tree nobody was there.

I heard a rustle. I looked up and there she was again, but further down the hill. Her red hair was thick with curls. My heart stopped. Could it be? She looked happy and was beckoning to me to follow her. It was a game of catch. She ran, so I ran faster – I had to catch up with her.

Then we started to go down, down another steep slope, weaving in and out of trees. The bracken scratched my legs and brambles caught at my clothes. It didn't matter. I was in a frenzy to touch her. To take hold of her. To beg forgiveness and ask 'why?'

As we came to the bottom of the hill, I saw she had reached a lake. She didn't hesitate. With one smooth movement, she walked right into the water. It didn't even occur to me to stop. Where she went I would follow.

I started walking into the water. I looked round frantically for her but I couldn't see her. I felt despair and desperation. The pain in my heart was paralysing. I screamed her name.

Suddenly, I heard shouting.

'Dolly!'

Was the voice coming from the lake? I walked further into the water.

'Dolly, no!'

I turned and saw a figure running towards me from the hospital.

'Dolly, don't! I'm coming to get you. Stay there! Don't go any further.'

I gazed at the man from what seemed like a huge distance, but I suddenly recognized Stanley.

I realized that I was waist deep in water and an undertow was pulling me further in. The lake seemed to want to devour me. I began to sink into the water and couldn't get back up for air. Under the water a hand moved towards me. I felt very calm. I reached for the hand, a white smooth hand. As I touched it, the hand took mine. I felt such joy. I felt a pull. I was being dragged along, then down.

I started to gasp for air. I could see silver bubbles streaming past me up towards the surface. We were spinning round.

I thought of Stanley being left behind. I thought of my dad blaming himself. I started to struggle. I didn't want to die! Suddenly the hold on my hand was released and I started fighting to get to the surface. It seemed to take for ever, but at last my head broke through the water and I took a deep gasp of air. I couldn't resist looking back. I saw my mother again, under the water, white, serene, floating. Why had she let me go? She could have taken me with her. But down she went, alone, her beautiful red hair billowing round her in the water. She looked up towards me with a soft smile and blew me a kiss. 'Catch it, Doll.'

I struggled to get to Stanley, who was up to his waist in the water and soaking wet. His shirt clung to him as he grabbed me and held me tight to his chest.

'You promised never to leave me,' he said. 'You promised.'

'And I never will,' I assured him.

We walked back up to the hospital where I dressed in dry clothes and packed my bag. I no longer needed to be surrounded by old people and the dying. I wanted to be loved. I wanted to live.

*

While I still felt as if a part of me was missing, I no longer felt numb. I was calm and knew that from now on I would remember the good things as well as the bad about my mother. I would be able to remember her as she was before her dreams soured her and life turned her into a bitter and twisted woman. I would remember her spinning in her red dress and laughingly blowing me kisses. 'Catch it, Doll.'

Chapter Twenty

We went back to my street that same afternoon. I stopped opposite the house and hesitated.

'Are you sure you want to do this?' Stanley asked me with his hand resting in the small of my back. 'We don't have to. We can go to mine. Dad's living with Mrs Dewsbury now at her house.'

I shook my head and carried on walking. 'No, this is right. You'll see, I'll be fine.'

We crossed the road. The cobbles reflected the light of the afternoon sun.

I stopped in front of the door. All the memories came flooding back. Me as a child sitting on the step. Me as a teenager trying to stop drunken men from entering the house. And me now, as a young woman in years but old before my time, hesitating before the door of the house where I killed my mum.

'I have to do this, Stanley,' I said, more to convince myself than him.

We went into the house, my house. The hallway was strangely light. The net curtains had been washed and the windows had been scrubbed until they sparkled.

The parlour door was open. I peered in. There were no heavy green curtains, just sunlight. No threadbare rug, or old worn-out sofa. They were all gone. Instead there was a deep red carpet and a new settee.

There was no smell of the tannery. The windows were wide open and a breeze blew through the entire house.

We carried on down the hall to the kitchen. We paused and looked at each other. Stanley took my hand in his and we opened the door and stepped through. We were greeted by a stream of sunlight. It lit up the clock on the mantelpiece and the silence was broken by the sound of kids playing in the street outside.

The range was the same, the table and chairs were the same, but it all looked lighter and cleaner, different.

'I came every day with your dad and we

cleaned and scrubbed, painted and repaired everything, just in case you wanted to come back.'

I looked at him and whispered, 'Thank you.'

I sat in my mum's chair by the range, and looked at the floor, where I had last seen her body. A feeling of sadness swept over me. What if things had been different? Was there anything I could have done? What if there hadn't been a war? Would that have changed things?

Stanley made a cup of tea and we sat in silence and thought about what could have been.

Upstairs was different too. Mum's bedroom had been cleared – it was totally empty. The bare floorboards had been swept and were clean.

My room was completely different too. Stanley had made it so comfy.

'I thought maybe you would like it this way. You don't mind, do you?' Stanley asked. He was so anxious to do the right thing. I just smiled and hugged him. My room was no longer a cold and dreary refuge. The walls had been painted yellow. There was a colourful bedspread on the bed and a cracked vase with some daisies in it on the windowsill. Stanley had brought the sun into my life.

That night we slept together in my room. As Stanley held me, I could feel him gently breathing. I felt a warmth and safety I knew would never leave me.

The next day I woke to find Stanley gone. I stared at his pillow. I dressed and went down to the kitchen, where the light, still as bright, flooded the room. The range was newly stoked, the kettle on the back keeping warm. There was a plate, a cup and saucer, milk and bread set out on the table.

There was also a note. Just as I was about to pick it up, there was a knock at the front door.

I was surprised. Had Stanley locked himself out?

The sun shone through the door so brightly, as I opened it, that I was blinded. For a moment, I saw a khaki uniform, a soldier come home again. But as my eyes grew accustomed to the light I saw Stanley standing there.

'Dolly, are you all right?' he asked. 'You look as if you'd seen a ghost.'

I fell into his arms, laughing. I hugged him tightly, out of relief more than anything else.

He lifted me up off the step into the hall. As he did I saw my dad's face smiling at me over Stanley's shoulder. He had a shy look on his face and he was wringing a new hat nervously in his hands.

'I've just been to fetch him from his digs,' Stanley explained. 'I said as soon as you were well enough I'd fetch him here to see you.'

Dad and I stared at each other.

'Princess,' he said nervously, looking at me with tears in his eyes.

I held out my hand and brought him into his house. It was a very different house now.

He was thin and pale.

'Princess, I never meant . . .'

I put my hand on his mouth and shook my head. He took me in his arms and we held each other and sobbed for the wasted years and the wasted lives.

A baby girl was born eight months later. We named her Daisy. I felt complete. Whatever had been missing from my life was made whole as soon as I looked into her big blue eyes.

Stanley and I got married as soon as I found out I was pregnant. We wanted her to have Stanley's name. My dad gave me away and even Stanley's father made an appearance at the wedding, accompanied by Mrs Dewsbury, no less.

There's no more smell of death in the house, only of life. The tannery was shut down and Dad found work elsewhere. He lives at home with me and Stanley now. You've never seen a more doting grandfather.

There are no cows screaming in the night. The only sound is that of laughter. As the sun sets in the evening, I sit out on the doorstep with little Daisy on my lap and we watch the other kids head for the welcoming fires of home. And I sing to her:

'The big ship sails on the ally-ally-oh,
The ally-ally-oh, the ally-ally-oh.
The big ship sails on the ally-ally-oh,
On the last day of September.'

Quick Reads

Books in the Quick Reads series

101 Ways to get your Child to Read	Patience Thomson
All These Lonely People	Gervase Phinn
Black-Eyed Devils	Catrin Collier
The Cave	Kate Mosse
Chickenfeed	Minette Walters
Cleanskin	Val McDermid
A Cool Head	Ian Rankin
Danny Wallace and the Centre of the Universe	Danny Wallace
The Dare	John Boyne
Doctor Who: I Am a Dalek	Gareth Roberts
Doctor Who: Made of Steel	Terrance Dicks
Doctor Who: Revenge of the Judoon	Terrance Dicks
Doctor Who: The Sontaran Games	Jacqueline Rayner
Dragons' Den: Your Road to Success	
A Dream Come True	Maureen Lee
Girl on the Platform	Josephine Cox
The Grey Man	Andy McNab
The Hardest Test	Scott Quinnell
Hell Island	Matthew Reilly
How to Change Your Life in 7 Steps	John Bird
Humble Pie	Gordon Ramsay
Life's New Hurdles	Colin Jackson
Lily	Adèle Geras
One Good Turn	Chris Ryan
RaW Voices: True Stories of Hardship	Vanessa Feltz
Reaching for the Stars	Lola Jaye
Reading My Arse!	Ricky Tomlinson
Star Sullivan	Maeve Binchy
The Sun Book of Short Stories	
Survive the Worst and Aim for the Best	Kerry Katona
The 10 Keys to Success	John Bird
The Tannery	Sherrie Hewson
Twenty Tales from the War Zone	John Simpson

Quick Reads

Pick up a book today

Quick Reads are bite-sized books by bestselling writers and well-known personalities for people who want a short, fast-paced read. They are designed to be read and enjoyed by avid readers and by people who never had or who have lost the reading habit.

Quick Reads are published alongside and in partnership with BBC RaW.

We would like to thank all our partners in the Quick Reads project for their help and support:

Arts Council England
The Department for Innovation, Universities and Skills
NIACE
unionlearn
National Book Tokens
The Vital Link
The Reading Agency
National Literacy Trust
Welsh Books Council
Basic Skills Cymru, Welsh Assembly Government
Wales Accent Press
The Big Plus Scotland
DELNI
NALA

Quick Reads would also like to thank the Department for Innovation, Universities and Skills; Arts Council England and World Book Day for their sponsorship and NIACE for their outreach work.

Quick Reads is a World Book Day initiative.
www.quickreads.org.uk www.worldbookday.com

Other resources

Free courses are available for anyone who wants to develop their skills. You can attend the courses in your local area. If you'd like to find out more, phone 0800 66 0800.

A list of books for new readers can be found on www.firstchoicebooks.org.uk or at your local library.

The
Vital
Link

Publishers Barrington Stoke (www.barringtonstoke.co.uk), New Island (www.newisland.ie) and Sandstone Press (www.sandstonepress.com) also provide books for new readers.

The BBC runs a reading and writing campaign. See www.bbc.co.uk/raw.

www.quickreads.org.uk

www.worldbookday.com